The little dragon was hot, steamy and
spiky; it had got its neck, wings, legs, claws,
tail, woven in and out of the bars like raffia
work, and trying to untangle it was like
trying to untangle a blackberry bush, but
Sam worked away patiently until he got the
squirmy, hooky little body safely down on
the grass.

At once the little dragon stopped bubbling
and steaming, and began to look pleased
and shiny. Its eye fell on Sam's blue lunch
box.

'What's that?' it asked.

WITHDRAWN FROM
THE LIBRARY
UNIVERSITY OF
WINCHESTER

'My lunch,' said Sam.

'Oh good,' said the dragon, and shot out a
tongue, flicked off the lid, and licked up
Sam's lunch, fast as fast, not a crumb
left . . .

One morning on the way to school Sam
rescues a young dragon trapped in the
chains of a swing. Scales – as the dragon is
called – decides to join Class 4 and he
brings lots of fun to Sam and his friends!

D1351936

Also available:

A DRAGON IN SPRING-TERM
A DRAGON IN SUMMER

A DRAGON IN CLASS 4

JUNE COUNSEL

YEARLING BOOKS

A DRAGON IN CLASS 4
A YEARLING BOOK 0 440 86267 1

First published in Great Britain by
Faber and Faber Ltd

PRINTING HISTORY
Faber and Faber edition published 1984
Young Corgi edition published 1986
Reprinted 1986, 1987, 1988 (twice), 1989
Reissued in Yearling edition 1991
Reprinted 1991 (twice), 1993

Text copyright © June Counsel 1984
Illustrations copyright © Faber and Faber 1984

Conditions of sale
1. This book is sold subject to the condition that it shall not, by
way of trade or otherwise, be lent, re-sold, hired out or otherwise
circulated without the publisher's prior consent in any form of
binding or cover other than that in which it is published and
without a similar condition including this condition being
imposed on the subsequent purchaser.

2. This book is sold subject to the Standard Conditions of Sale of
Net Books and may not be re-sold in the UK below the net price
fixed by the publishers for the book.

This book was set in 14/16 pt Century Schoolbook by
Chippendale Type Ltd., Otley, West Yorkshire.

Yearling Books are published by Transworld Publishers Ltd.,
61–63 Uxbridge Road, Ealing, London W5 5SA, in
Australia by Transworld Publishers (Australia) Pty. Ltd.,
15–25 Helles Avenue, Moorebank, NSW 2170, and in
New Zealand by Transworld Publishers (N.Z.) Ltd.,
3 William Pickering Drive, Albany, Auckland.

Printed and bound in Great Britain by
Cox & Wyman Ltd., Reading, Berks.

KING ALFRED'S COLLEGE
WINCHESTER

SCHOOL RESOURCES CENTRE

CF/COU   01549804

*For my past and present friends
at Walton Infant School*

Contents

1 Can't You Spell?

Mooching along the lane to school one miserable Monday morning, Sam caught a glitter of movement out of the corner of his eye. Something unusual and brightly coloured was happening at the far end of the Rec where the baby swings stood. Although he was late and spelling was the first lesson, Sam couldn't help but go across to see what it was, and when he did see what it was—

'My word!' said Sam. 'My very, very, word!'

For it was a dragon, a small dragon, tangled up in the bars of the baby swings, bubbling like a saucepan!

'Stop tying yourself up like a parcel,' commanded Sam, putting down his lunch box, 'and I'll untie you!'

The little dragon was hot, steamy and spiky; it had got its neck, wings, legs, claws, tail, woven in and out of the bars like raffia work, and trying to untangle it was like trying to untangle a blackberry bush, but Sam

worked away patiently until he got the squirmy, hooky little body safely down on the grass.

At once the little dragon stopped bubbling and steaming and began to look pleased and shiny. Its eye fell on Sam's blue lunch box.

'What's that?' it asked.

'My lunch,' said Sam.

'Oh good,' said the dragon, and shot out a tongue, flicked off the lid, and licked up Sam's lunch, fast as fast, not a crumb left.

'Hey!' cried Sam. 'That was my lunch! Good job I've got a banana in my pocket. You've scoffed the lot!'

'Dragons do,' said the dragon. 'My dad can scoff twenty cows at a lick.' It poked Sam's legs with its sharp snout. 'Are you real?'

'Course I'm real,' said Sam angrily. 'I was real enough to get you out of that swing, wasn't I? Now I'm going to be late for school *and* you've scoffed my lunch *and* it's spelling.'

'Can't you spell?' said the dragon in amazement.

'No,' said Sam shortly, 'I always come bottom.'

'You must be dim,' said the dragon astonished. 'I can spell anything.'

'Spell Tyrannosaurus Rex then,' challenged Sam.

'Simp,' said the dragon. 'T Y R A double N O S A U R U S space REX. Even baby dragons can spell that.'

Sam was dumbfounded, but before he could speak the church clock began to strike nine, and with a yelp he began to run. 'Oh, golly Moses me, I'm going to be late!'

'Don't worry, I'll look after you. I've always wanted a boy of my own,' cried the dragon, bounding along beside him. 'Jump on my back, I'll whoosh you to school.'

Sam flung himself on between two of its spines, and the long lane to school went flying by him like a ball of wool unwinding. Next minute he was rolling over and over in the school yard, just as Miss Green finished ringing the bell.

'Well, good gracious, Sam,' said Miss Green, looking down on him, 'what a way to come to school! Did you come on a bicycle? You must take more care!' Sam picked himself up and followed her in. He was so dazed he forgot to take his banana out of his coat pocket. The little dragon was nowhere to be seen, but Miss Green was opening windows and taking her cardigan off. 'It's very warm,' she said.

There was a great bunch of autumn foliage on the Nature Table, golden beech leaves, scarlet rosehips, crimson haws from the hawthorn trees. Suddenly, with no-one near it, the table wobbled.

13

'Now then,' said Miss Green, 'while our brains are fresh this lovely autumn morning, spelling! We'll have all our old tricky friends.' Sam saw a sharp golden snout poke through the beech leaves and two blackberry-bright eyes looked at him through the rosehips. One of them winked. 'Try your hardest, Sam. If you get just one right, I'll be pleased with you. I'll say each word twice.'

Sam sighed. You can say them ten times, he thought, and I'll still get them wrong. It's not *saying* them that helps, it's *seeing* them.

'They,' began Miss Green. She put her tongue between her teeth. '*They.*'

Sam looked at her sadly. Inside Miss Green's head were the right spellings, but he couldn't see inside Miss Green's head. Then, an extra-ordinary thing happened. A speech bubble came out of Miss Green's lips. She brushed her hand across her lips as though she were brushing away a hair.

The bubble floated over to Sam. It

had little black tadpoles swimming in it. The tadpoles caught hold of each other's tails and turned into fat black letters. There was a *t*, an *h*, an *e* and a *y*. The bubble burst and the fat black letters fell down on to Sam's paper. No-one else noticed anything. The *e* was a great show-off, it kept turning somersaults to attract attention. Sam laughed. Miss Green looked up. At once the letters lay down flat, the *t* first, then the *h*, *e* third and *y* last. They shrivelled and vanished. Sam wrote down *they* and made a very black, thick e in the middle.

'Was,' went on Miss Green, *'was.'*

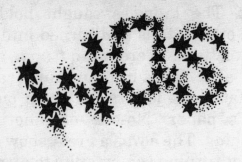

Another bubble blew out from her lips, blue as the sky. She flicked it away, and it floated over to Sam and burst into shining stars. The stars ran together into glittering letters, a *w* and an *a* and an *s*, and settled gently on Sam's page. The *w* lay still, but the *a* and the *s* rolled about as though it were a great joke to be in *was* at all. Sam put his hand over them to keep them still and felt them tickle, like a shrimp he had once caught at the seaside. When he took his hand away, they vanished. He wrote down *was* with an *a*, and an *s*.

'Down,' continued Miss Green. *'Down.'*

An aeroplane zoomed out of her mouth, dropped four letters by parachute and exploded. The letters touched down on the head of the girl in front. They formed up and began to march down her pigtails in single file. 'There's a fly on my hair,' said the girl, shaking them off, but not before Sam had noticed their marching order, and seen that the *w* came before the *n*.

'Talk,' Miss Green was saying, '*talk*. You should all get that right. You do enough of it!'

Out of her mouth came a yellow post office van. It sped over to Sam's desk, flung out four little red telephones and hurtled away. The telephones untangled their flexes, which turned into little red letters, a *t* and an *a* and an *l* and a *k*, and all four began to ring each other up and talk in tiny crackling voices.

'Ssh!' said Miss Green, looking over at Sam.

'Ssh!' said Sam to the telephones. They stopped talking and vanished. Where they had been, Sam wrote down *talk* with an *al* in the middle.

So it went on. It was the first spelling test Sam had ever enjoyed. It wasn't easy, though. The letters had so much bounce and character. The word 'jump' came out as four splendid showjumpers, and even when the horses turned into letters they still went on jumping. The *m* with its three legs was particularly good. Sam had to put his ruler across them to keep them still. But he remembered to put the *m* in '*jump*'.

'And now,' said Miss Green, 'just for fun and to end with, elephant! *Elephant!*'

This'll be fun, thought Sam, to see an elephant come out of Miss Green's mouth. But nothing came out of Miss Green's mouth. No speech bubble, nothing! Sam was aghast. He looked at the Nature Table. Not a leaf moved. He looked round the room.

Through the archway, in the bay where the big playthings were kept, a baby elephant was putting on a pink top hat with the letters *e l e* in silver on the front. Beside it crouched the little dragon busily tying a broad pink ribbon round its middle. The ribbon had a big *ph* on it in silver.

19

The dragon gave the baby elephant a little push to turn it round and fixed the pink bow on the end of its tail with three letters hanging from it. Sam laughed. Fancy great big enormous *elephant* ending in tiny, little *ant*! He wrote it down. When he looked again the bay was empty.

'Papers in,' called Miss Green, 'and everyone have a rest.'

Phew! thought Sam, what a lesson! He felt suddenly hungry. Good job I've got my banana.

'Sam,' cried Miss Green. 'Wonderful boy! You have got every one right! A great big, enormous clap for Sam, everybody!'

Sam stood by Miss Green's desk staring at his spelling paper with the red ticks going all down the page and the gold star shining at the bottom. Generous Class 4 clapped like mad and he knew he was grinning like an idiot. He looked hard at the Nature Table, but it held only leaves and berries and branches. He raised his eyes to the window and saw far away on the other side of the playing field a baby elephant in a top hat and a small dragon walking together under the golden autumn trees. The dragon seemed to be offering the elephant a banana.

2 Sep-Dibby-Di-Dum

Sam was so puffed up with his spelling success that he asked Miss Green if he could take his reading book home.

'I want to amaze you,' he told her.

'I'm not supposed to let reading books go home,' said Miss Green, 'but if you want to amaze me, by all means. Don't let it get dirty, and bring it back tomorrow.'

Sam took the book down to the garden shed and began to read. It grew very warm and he took his jumper off. It grew warmer still and he looked up. There stood the little dragon, puffing warm breath at him.

'Oh good,' it said, 'you're still real.'

'Of course I'm real,' said Sam. 'I'm trying to read. Trouble is I read so slowly I forget what the last word was before I've read the next.'

'I'm a wiz at reading,' said the little dragon. 'I'll teach you to read so fast you'll know the last word before you've read the first! What's your name?'

'Sam,' said Sam. 'What's yours?'

'Scales,' said the little dragon, 'that's my nickname, but my *real* name is Sep-dibby-di-dum. If you ever need me *desperately* you may say it, but not otherwise, because it's magic. Now give us your reading book.'

They settled themselves on a roll of old stair-carpet and began. Scales had a wonderful way with words. He could make them jump off the page and hit you in the eye. And once

they'd done that, you never forgot
what they meant.

'I want to amaze Miss Green,' Sam
told Scales.

'You'll amaze her all right,' said
that confident dragon. 'She'll blow up
with amazement, I shouldn't wonder.'

Next morning Sam went bouncing
joyfully along the lane with his reading book in one hand and his lunch
box in the other, happily picturing
Miss Green's amazement when he

read his reading book to her, word perfect.

A sharp pain began in his ear and another in his wrist.

'Ow!' yelled Sam. 'Get off, Pincher, let go, leave me alone.'

Pincher was a Junior boy who preyed on Infants. His grinning face came closer, his dirty nails did not let go. 'Ooer! We've been taking our reading book home to practise! That's not allowed. We might get them dirty!' He twisted the reading book out of Sam's hand and held it up in the air. As Sam jumped to get it, Pincher sent it spinning down the lane. It fell splash into a puddle. Sam turned to get it and Pincher jerked his lunch box from him. 'Ooer! Chocolate biscuits. Two of them. One for us and one for a friend!' He crammed the biscuits into his mouth and threw the lunch box over the hedge. Sam tried to dodge round him, but Pincher flickered about him like a darning needle. Suddenly he dived both hands into Sam's pockets. 'Ooer! What have we here? Dinner money and bank money! Ooer!' Too much for little Sammy to carry. Sammy could lose them, or forget them.' He stuffed both envelopes into his torn trouser pocket. His sharp eyes stared at Sam. His voice hissed. 'Don't you tell it was me. You tell anyone it was me and I'll pinch you to pieces.' He shot off and the lane was empty.

Sam went back and picked up his reading book. He tried to wipe the mud and water off it with his sleeve, but he only smeared the pages. He trudged on to school, shaking with rage and misery.

'Oh, my goodness!' cried Miss Green. 'A boy of your age to go falling into puddles! I don't know how I'm going to get this book clean. Where's your dinner money and your bank? H'm? You forgot? Well, you shouldn't forget. You should remember. I have to remember,' said Miss Green.

It was a miserable morning. No lunch made Sam feel empty and cold. When Miss Green fetched his reading book from the radiator where she had put it to dry, he could only stare at it dumbly. He knew the words, Scales had seen to that, but they didn't seem real any more.

'Never mind, Sam,' said Miss Green. 'We'll try again tomorrow.'

In the dinner hour Sam stood miserably by himself, thinking with dread of the long walk home when school ended. His flesh ached as though Pincher's fingers were already at work on it. Suddenly Pincher himself came leaping over the fence that separated the Junior School from the Infants and ran straight to where the baby class was playing. His arm came up, his hand opened, something flew from it. There was a bang, a

flash, screams, cries. Children ran about knocking each other over. He had thrown a firecracker among them.

The dinner women came charging over. Pincher ran for the gate. Sam spread out his arms to catch him. Pincher knocked him over. 'Sep-dibby-di-dum,' breathed Sam, flat on his back, seeing stars. There was a rush and a roar. Pincher came tearing

back from the gate, both hands clutching his bottom. 'Get it off me! Get it off! It's burning my bum!' He ran slap into the arms of the dinner women, who marched him off to Miss Green.

Miss Green was in the middle of marking and very angry at being disturbed. 'What nonsense is this? A dragon chased you? Breathing fire? It burnt your bottom? Well, let me tell you, I shall breathe fire and burn your bottom if you come into the Infants' playground again. What's this?' She pulled at an envelope with Sam's name on it sticking out of Pincher's torn trouser pocket. 'This is Sam Luckett's dinner money, and his bank money! Just how, pray, did they come to be in your pocket?'

After that things got worse and worse for Pincher. He was hauled away and led before the Headmaster of the Juniors, a terrible man with evildoers. But they got better and better for Sam. Miss Green called him in and gave him back his bank book and dinner money. 'I can guess now who spoiled your reading book,' she said. 'It was Pincher, wasn't it?' Sam nodded. Miss Green led him to her cupboard, unlocked it, and took out a brand new reading book and handed it to Sam. 'Let's try again,' she said.

Sam opened the shining pages, so stiff they would hardly turn, took a deep breath and began to read. Miss

Green listened, and her eyes grew bigger and bigger and bigger. 'Sam, you amaze me,' she said when he finished. 'I never thought you could read like that. Well done!'

Sam walked home along the lane, whistling. He climbed through the hedge and found his lunch box. It was undamaged and had a snail in it. 'I'll take you home,' said Sam, who liked snails. He felt as happy as a king. If Pincher ever came for him again, he knew how to deal with him. But, strange to say, Pincher never did.

3   Scales Takes Over

'There was a dragon in the playground yesterday,' Class 4 told Miss Green. 'Wasn't just Pincher who saw it. We did too. Well, some of us did. Well, one of us did.'

'I saw it,' said Italian Tina, 'a bambino dragon chasing Pincher with fire in its mouth.'

'All imagination,' said Miss Green, 'but it's nice to think of Pincher getting his just desserts for once. He's been a nuisance to us for far too long.' She sounded tired and her face looked white and drawn. 'Class 4,' she said, 'I don't know how we're going to do it, but we have got to get our wall picture up by Friday.'

'We'll never do it,' said Weefy Buffalo. 'Today's Wednesday and we haven't even started.'

'I know,' said Miss Green. She dragged herself up. 'Sam, dear, go and fetch some paper from the bay.'

It was warm in the bay with the sun shining through the window. Sam knelt by the big chest where the paper was kept and felt heat on his back. 'Is she real?' asked Scales in his ear. 'She looks like a ghost.'

'Of course she's real,' said Sam, 'but she's got one of her heads, that's why she's so pale.'

'How many heads has she got?' asked Scales excitedly. 'There's an ogre near us who's got . . . '

'Don't be silly,' said Sam. 'I mean she's got one of her headaches. Miss Green gets very bad headaches.'

'All those children in there,' went on Scales, 'are they real?'

'For goodness sake,' said Sam, 'of course they're real, as you'd jolly soon know if you got among them.'

He stood up with his arms full of paper. 'We've got to get our wall picture up by Friday and it's Wednesday now. Class 5 have got theirs up already.'

'So?' said Scales. 'What's the fuss? You've got three days.'

'The fuss,' said Sam, 'is that we haven't even thought what to paint yet and it takes days to paint a wall picture.'

'Let me do it,' said Scales immediately. 'I'm brill at painting. Get Miss Green out of the way and I'll paint you a wall picture before you can say Rolf Harris.'

'Miss Green,' said Sam, 'why don't you lie down on the daybed in the bay and shut your eyes? We can stick the paper together for the wall picture. We know how to do it.'

'Yes,' cried Class 4, clustering

round her. 'We've done it before. You go and lie down and we'll be very quiet, very QUIET!' they shouted.

'Oh my goodness,' moaned poor Miss Green, putting her hands to her head. 'Very well then. You're sensible children. But I shan't be asleep. I shall just have my eyes shut and I shall hear if anyone's being silly.'

So Class 4 led her off to the bay and laid her tenderly on the daybed and covered her up with blankets from the Wendy House. Miss Green had made the daybed herself on a woodwork course and it was strong and comfortable.

'Thank you, children,' she murmured with her eyes closed. 'I shall be all right soon. Oh, what lovely warmth! Like a hotwater bottle! I shan't go to sleep, mind . . . I shall just have my eyes closed . . .'

Her voice trailed off, there was a gentle snore, and Miss Green was asleep!

'That's fixed her,' said Scales briskly. He left off breathing warm air over her and whisked into the classroom, where he hopped up on to her desk.

'I'm Scales,' he announced. 'I'm going to paint a picture not by numbers but by seconds! Stand back, everybody, and watch!'

Class 4 stared at him with its mouth open, but Weefy Buffalo found words. 'Oh no, you aren't,' he said. 'You may be Sam's dragon, but this is our painting and we're going to do it!'

'I am *not* Sam's dragon,' hissed Scales, swelling with rage. 'Sam is *my* boy!'

'You're very bossy,' said little Tina. 'You make much with the mouth, no?'

'Of course I'm bossy,' said Scales. 'All dragons are bossy. You can't be feeble-minded if you're a dragon.'

'Be quiet, Scales,' said Sam. 'What we've got to decide is not who's going to paint, but what we're going to paint.'

'Me!' cried Scales.

'Scales!' cried Class 4.

So there was no argument about that!

'Right,' said Scales, stretching himself out full length on the paper. 'Now, draw round me!'

It took a lot of drawing to draw round Scales. There were so many ups and downs and ins and outs and curves and wiggles.

'This is complicated,' said Weefy Buffalo, as he broke his pencil point trying to steer it between two spines.

'Are you real?' asked Scales, looking up at him. Weefy was a very odd-looking boy.

'I'm real,' murmured Weefy Buffalo, bending over him, 'question is, are you?'

At last they were done. Scales sprang off the paper. 'A-a-h,' cried Class 4, 'have we done that?' For there before them on the paper lay the most lifelike outline of a dragon.

'One hardly needs teachers,' murmured clever Christopher. 'One wonders why they don't become extinct.'

'Now then,' said Scales quickly,

before anyone could butt in, 'everyone wearing yellow, do my throat and tummy yellow. Everyone wearing black, paint my eyes and claws black. Everyone wearing red, colour my spines and crest red, and my tongue, of course. Everyone wearing purple — is anyone wearing purple? ('I'm wearing purple,' said little Tina) — do the purple spike on my tail and the purple tufts above my eyes. Everyone wearing green do my sides and tail green.'

'What about us?' called a lot of disgruntled voices. 'What do we paint?'

'Dull earthy browns and dreary greys do the background,' said Scales loftily. 'Rocks, earth and charred trees.'

Class 4 dipped their brushes and flew at the paper. Colours glowed like Scales' own colours, battle-red, brassy yellow, plum-purple and polished pepper-green. Scales hopped round exhorting them. 'More red, more yellow, more purple, more green. Make me fiercer, make me bigger, make me stupendous.'

It was finished. A huge dragon, wings raised, claws extended, jaws gaping, blazed along the paper looking as though it could eat the world. Behind it lay a sombre background of broken rock, scorched earth and blackened trees.

'Terrif!' cried Scales. 'I'm a genius.'

'You?' cried Class 4. 'We did all the work!'

'Children,' came a drowsy voice from the bay. 'The bell will be going soon. Tidy up now and pack away!'

Class 4 stared at each other. Tidy up! Pack away! Before the bell? Impossible! There was paint on the floor, paint on the walls, paint on the tables and chairs. There was paint on their hands, paint on their clothes, paint on their faces and hair. Never could they clean it up.

'But I can,' said Scales, reading their thoughts. 'I can clean the whole room before you count ten.'

'One, two three . . . ' began Class 4 as Scales whirled round the room, 'four, five, six,' nearly twisting their heads off as their eyes followed Scales, 'seven, eight, nine . . . ' but it was done. Floors, walls, chairs, tables spotless, brushes back in pots, pots back in sink and Scales back on Miss Green's desk, his face glossy with conceit.

The daybed creaked. They could hear Miss Green reaching for her handbag. 'But what about us?' said Class 4's eyes to Scales.

'Fret not,' said Scales, sliding over. 'I'll give you a dragon wash. Stand still, don't squeak.' It felt like a hot rough flannel, a gust of warm air, and a scratchy comb. 'There,' said Scales. He scooted across to the Nature Table and disappeared just as a pink, happy-faced Miss Green came through the archway.

'Children, you have been good. We'll make a start on the picture tomorr . . . good gracious me! Did you do that? You clever, clever children, and not a speck of paint anywhere. I *am* pleased!'

'It's Sam's dragon,' said Class 4, proudly.

The Nature Table shook violently and two conkers rolled off.

'Sam's his boy,' said Weefy quickly.

'Ah,' said Miss Green. 'Is he?' She looked hard at the dragon picture. 'Well, there's only one word for him. He is . . . stupendous!'

4 Sebastian and the Weatherboard

'All right,' said Miss Green. 'I give in. Sam really has got a dragon, its name is Scales and you've all seen it.'

'Yes,' said Class 4. 'We all have.'

'I haven't,' smiled Sebastian, a tiresome boy.

'You were away yesterday,' Miss Green told him. 'Well, Scales has certainly improved your stories, Class 4. They are very good, but why did nobody use the word big or come up to me for the word fierce?'

'Because Scales isn't big or fierce,' said Class 4. 'He's little and bossy and bouncy, just like a teacher, and full of super ideas.'

'Thank you,' said Miss Green. 'Compliments always welcome. Well, shall we think some more about dragons? Where do they live?'

'In caves!' shouted Class 4.

'In caves they do,' nodded Miss Green, 'and as we are going to do magic *e* this morning, we'll start with a nice big rocky cave.'

She moved across to the blackboard and Class 4 settled down to enjoy themselves (Miss Green was a super drawer) when Sebastian put his hand up.

'We haven't done the Weatherboard yet,' he said.

'Nor we have,' Miss Green said. 'Thank you, Sebastian. Jump up, Sam, it's your turn.'

'But it's my turn,' said Sebastian smugly.

'It's not,' said Sam angrily.

'It is,' said Sebastian.

Miss Green looked at the chart called 'My Helpers' which hung by the door. 'It does say Sebastian,' she said in puzzled tones. 'I could have sworn I put Sam's name there.'

'You did,' said Sam. 'It's my turn. I know it is.'

'But here is Sebastian's name opposite Weatherboard,' went on Miss Green, 'so hop up, Sebastian, and do it. I'm sorry, Sam. It's all this talk of dragons that's making us muddly.'

'It hasn't muddled me,' said Sebastian. 'I don't believe in dragons.'

'I'm sure you don't,' said Miss Green. 'Now, the rest of us, let's look at this word "cave".'

Sebastian got up, adjusting his bow tie with a self-satisfied smirk. Sam sat silent, seething with rage. He knew his name had been up. He'd seen it up yesterday.

'When we've done our writing,' said Miss Green with a glance at Sam's furious face, 'we'll clear the things off the Measuring Table and make a cave there. We'll get black, brown and grey paper, crunch it up and stick it all over the biggest box we can find. We'll make a cave on a lonely waste by the waves of the sea,' said Miss Green, getting carried away.

'I've done the Weatherboard,' said Sebastian, holding it up. He was a lad who liked a lot of praise.

'Sunny?' said Miss Green. 'But it isn't sunny, Sebastian! Look out of the window. It's raining!'

'But it was bright sunshine when we came to school!' squeaked Sebastian.

'Well, it isn't now,' said Miss Green. 'It's pouring cats and dogs. So change it, please. Now, everybody, who wants to glue, who wants to crunch paper, who wants to mix paints, who wants to find boxes?' A forest of arms waved about her and a babel of voices rose in the air. Gradually Class 4 divided itself into groups; some went into the bay to get paper, some went in search of boxes, some began to mix paint. Sam helped Miss Green clear the Measuring Table.

'Can I help now, Miss Green?' asked Sebastian, coming up. 'I've put raining in.'

Miss Green glanced briefly out of the window. 'The rain's stopped,' she said. 'Look how those tree-tops are bending! Put "windy", Sebastian. We'd better get it right. Suppose Miss Barley were to come in?'

Muttering under his breath and scowling hard, Sebastian went back to the Weatherboard and began to search for the word 'windy' and the picture of the little girl with the umbrella blown inside out.

'Gracious, what a lot of boxes,' said Miss Green. 'I think what we'll do is stick several of them together to build up a jaggedy, rocky mountain and then have this big box in front for the cave.'

Soon Class 4 was up to its eyebrows in glue, paper, scissors and boxes. Sam had got over his disappointment and was cutting thin, wavy strips of silver foil to look like trickles of water seeping down between rocks.

Everyone had forgotten Sebastian when he suddenly cried out, 'Now can I join in, Miss Green? I've put "windy" in the right picture. Look!' Class 4 looked across at the Weatherboard and then out of the window.

'But I cannot see the trees at all,' cried little Tina.

'Nor the houses opposite,' cried Weefy Buffalo.

'Not even the railings,' cried Sam.

'Looks like you're going to have to change it again,' laughed clever Christopher. 'Take out "windy", Sebastian, and put in "foggy", because that's what it undoubtedly is.'

'Yes,' said Miss Green kindly, seeing how staggered Sebastian looked. 'We shall look very silly having "windy" on our Weatherboard if all the other classes have "foggy".'

Sebastian's face grew black as thunder. For a moment it looked as if he were going to hurl the Weatherboard to the floor and jump on it, but he did not. He hunched round, stamped over to the Weather Table and began sorting through the box of wooden words and pictures with a great clatter.

'Look at this, Class 4,' cried Miss Green. 'This is beginning to look something like a cave! Put the lights on, please, Sebastian, it's got very dark.'

'I suppose you'll all agree that it's right now?' shouted Sebastian, spinning round with 'foggy' in the Weatherboard and the swirly picture of fog above it.

'Look out of the window and check,' said Miss Green, down among the glue-pots and the growing pile of life-like rocks. 'We're all busy, but mind you get it right.'

Sebastian pushed his way through the painters and stickers to the window. There came a loud wail and a crash as he hurled the Weatherboard to the floor.

'It's snowing!' he shrieked. 'It *keeps* changing. It's doing it on purpose!' He flung himself down at a table and sobbed with fury and frustration. Class 4 stared at him, shocked. Sebastian was always tiresome, but nobody liked to see him cry. It made them feel uncomfortable.

Miss Green went quickly over to him. 'Don't be silly, Sebastian,' she said, putting an arm round his shoulders. 'It's very changeable at this time of year. Though, I must say, I didn't expect snow.'

'It's because I changed the name-card,' sobbed Sebastian. 'I took Sam's name out this morning when you weren't looking and put mine in, and now it's punishing me.'

'Nothing is punishing you,' cried Miss Green, 'but your own prickly conscience, and I'm very glad to see it is. What a sneaky thing to do! Go and put Sam's name back at once, and then come and say you're sorry to Sam.'

Sebastian, looking damp, went sulkily over to the Helpers Chart, took his name-card out of the elastic loops, and put Sam's name-card in opposite Weatherboard.

'Now, Sam,' said Miss Green, 'you look out of the window and tell us what the weather's doing.'

Sam walked over to the window. 'Cor!' he said. Snowflakes like tiny ballerinas were pirouetting down from the skies. The yard was white with them.

Sebastian came and stood beside him. 'Sorry, Sam,' he mumbled. The snowflakes stopped, the sun came out, and the snow ran away in streams of sparkling silver. Sam felt a great warmth in his heart.

'It's sunny,' he said, and went and put 'sunny' in the Weatherboard.

'Can I help with the cave now?' pleaded Sebastian, looking at Miss Green without any of his usual cockiness.

'I'm afraid it's finished,' said Miss Green, 'but you can help Sam lift it up on to the Measuring Table, because you two are my strong chaps. The rest of you tidy up, because the bell will be going.'

So Sam and Sebastian heaved the cave up on to the table and put stones and withered leaves from the Nature Table before it. It looked a bare, desolate place. The bell rang and Miss Green picked up her handbag.

'Everyone out,' she said. 'Sam, you and Sebastian finish tidying up and then go out to play.'

'Scales would like this cave,' said Sam. 'It was he who changed the weather. He can do magic.'

Sebastian tried to smile disbelievingly, but he couldn't quite manage it. He bent down and peered into the cave's dark mouth. A gust of warm air struck him on the face and he jumped back.

'I believe in you, Scales,' he called.
Scales' voice said, 'Super cave, Sam! Thanks a lot. But as for you, Sebastian of the Bow Tie, you're going to have to change your ways, considerably, my lad, before *I* believe in *you*.'

5   Aunt Spiny

'I'm going to live in that cave,' said Scales to Sam the next day. 'It's going to be my hideaway place.'

'You can come home with me,' said Sam, who rather fancied another ride on Scales.

'Thank you, no,' said Scales. 'I want to stay with Class 4. They're fun.'

They were in the bay washing out paint pots. The school had been built long ago and there wasn't room in the classrooms now for all the new things that had to be kept in them. So each classroom had an extra bit out from it into the yard, which was called the bay. The bays had sinks in them and large windows that let in the sunshine. Best of all, unless Miss Green came and looked through the archway, you couldn't be seen in the bay.

'I told my mum about you,' said Scales, cleaning the inside of a paint pot with his tongue, 'and she said all small dragons have imaginary playmates.'

'My dad says dragons don't exist,' said Sam, taking the paint pot from Scales and rinsing it under the tap.

'My dad says schoolteachers are mythical beasts,' said Scales.

'Our dads are wrong,' said Sam, who knew that Miss Green was not a beast, and felt sure that she wasn't mythical. 'What does your dad do?'

'Ordinary things,' said Scales, starting on another paint pot. 'He lays waste, and devours maidens, and guards treasure.'

'What's laying waste mean?' asked Sam.

'Oh, trampling about, burning up trees, licking up cows.'

'And what's devouring maidens?' asked Sam.

'Maidens are girls,' replied Scales. 'My dad has to eat them. That's what "devour" means.'

'He doesn't,' cried Sam, shocked.

'He does,' replied Scales, 'he has to. People bring them to him specially and beg him to. He puts them in his mouth like this,' said Scales, putting a paintbrush in his mouth, 'and swallows them down in one go.' The paintbrush went down in one go. 'That way he doesn't taste them.'

Sam was silent. Scales looked at him. 'They don't feel anything,' he said. 'They go giggle, giggle, giggle, eek! And that's it.'

'Have you finished washing the paint pots, Sam?' called Miss Green. 'There seems to be a lot of talking going on in the bay.'

'Just finishing,' Sam called.

'Then dry your hands and come along. We're just going to unroll the magic mat.'

The magic mat was an old carpet from Miss Green's home, with a faded flowery pattern on it, on which Class 4 sat for storytime.

'Please,' called Sam. 'Could Scales tell the story today? He's got a very interesting family.'

'If Scales *can* tell a story, yes,' said Miss Green. 'I want to tidy my cupboard, but remember, although I shall be on the other side of the room with my back to you, I shall be listening, and if anyone's silly . . . '

'No-one will be silly with me!' said Scales in Sam's voice, and he sat down on the magic mat and Class 4 settled round him.

'This is a story about my Aunt Spiny,' began Scales. 'My Aunt Spiny is a widow dragon. She lives with us with all her children. I've got more cousins,' said Scales, gloomily staring at Sebastian, 'than you've got bow ties.' Sebastian wore a different bow tie every week. 'And, golly, they are *silly*. Well, my dad is huge, my mum is big, but my Aunt Spiny is tiny. That is, tiny for a dragon. She's about as big as four of those tables pushed together.'

'Gracious,' exclaimed Class 4, who didn't think that tiny at all.

'But, although she's tiny, she's fierce! One day when we were all at sixes and sevens in our cave, my mum poorly, my dad nursing a wound he'd got in a fight, my silly cousins squabbling, and my Aunt Spiny rushing round looking after the lot of us, a man came up our mountain waving a sword and challenged my dad to a fight.

' "I'm wounded," called my father from the back of the cave. "Come back next week."

' "I want your golden treasure," shouted the man. "So you come out and fight."

'Everybody knows my dad guards treasure. "Fair's fair," called my

father. "I'll fight when I'm fit."

'The man began calling names, and I grew angry. "I'll go," I said.

' "No, no," said my father, struggling up, "he'd fry you for breakfast. I'll go."

' "No, no," cried my mother, rolling over, "you're hurt. I'll go."

' "No, no," cried all my silly cousins, "you're not well. We'll go."

' "SIT DOWN THE LOT OF YOU," roared my Aunt Spiny. "I'LL GO!"

'So we sat down, the lot of us, and my Aunt Spiny went, and when the man saw her, he laughed so much he fell off his horse, and it galloped off down the mountainside. It didn't like the smell of dragon and it was bothered by there not being any fresh grass. There isn't any fresh grass round our cave, on account of my dad laying waste.

' "Why, you scaly old worm," shouted the man to my Aunt Spiny. "I could skewer you on my sword and wave you round my head."

'Aunt Spiny looked down at him. For all his fighting words he hadn't come right up to the cave. He was still some way below her.

' "Don't kill me," said my Aunt Spiny in a thin, grey voice like a cobweb talking, "spare my life and I will give you the greatest treasure a man can wish for."

' "Kill you!" cried the man, shaking with laughter. "There'd be no glory in killing an old bootlace like you! I'll just come up and tickle your throat with my sword."

' "Just come up then," said Aunt

Spiny, her voice quivering like a cob-web with a fly on it, "and do that."

'So the man began to come up the slope towards her, whistling and smiling and swinging his sword round his head. He didn't even bother to put his visor down to protect his face. But as he came nearer he stopped whistling. Then, he stopped smiling. Then, he stopped swinging his sword. Then . . . he stopped altogether. His armour began to rattle. His knees began to shake, and his voice, when he could find it, shook too.

' "Wh-wh-what are you d-d-doing? Wh-wh-what's happening?"

'For my Aunt Spiny was swelling! She was swelling and swelling and swelling! It's a trick dragons do to frighten their enemies. She blew herself up until she was four times her natural size. Her crest stood up like spikes and the frill round her neck that usually lay flat reared up like a huge steel ruff. Her scales turned black and crimson, and when she next spoke her voice hissed like rain falling on hot earth.

' "Closer, closer," hissed Aunt Spiny, "closer if you are going to tickle my throat with your sword."

' "I-I've changed my mind," stammered the man. "I-I've d-d-decided to s-s-spare your life! J-j-just give me the treasure and I'll go. Y-y-you promised, you know."

' "Yessss!" hissed my Aunt Spiny, "but keep your word to me first! Tickle my throat with your sword.

You said you would, you know! Look, I'll help you!" She opened her terrible jaws and he saw the fires flickering at the back of her throat.

'How that man moved himself forward I'll never know,' said Scales. 'My silly cousins and I were peering from the mouth of the cave. But he did. With his sword arm stretched before him as far as it would go and his sword shaking like a branch in the wind, he inched forward.

' "Nearer than that," said my Aunt Spiny softly.

'So he came nearer than that.

' "Nearer yet," crooned my Aunt Spiny.

'So he came nearer yet.

' "Nearer," whispered my Aunt Spiny.

'So he came nearer.

'SNAP! Aunt Spiny caught his sword arm, encased in mail, in her teeth. She didn't bite it off. She held it, while inside her mouth the sword in his shaking hand tickled her throat. "A-a-ah!" smiled my Aunt Spiny, "that's nice." And every tooth in her long, long smile glistened at the man.

'She bit off the sword just below the hilt and crunched it up. "Best British steel," she said, licking her lips. "I haven't tasted that for years." And she looked greedily at his armour.

' "The treasure!" whispered the man, whitefaced. "You promised!"

' "So I did," said my Aunt Spiny regretfully. "Take it then!" And she flipped him over backwards and sent him rolling down the mountainside.

' "But what have you given me?" wailed the man as he bounced from rock to rock, clutching his swordhilt and nothing else.

' "YOUR LIFE!" roared Aunt Spiny. "The greatest treasure any man, or dragon, can have!"

'LIFE! LIFE! Life! Life!, echoed the mountain as the man rolled down it. We heard him get on his horse at the bottom and gallop away. My Aunt Spiny let the air out of herself and came back into the cave.'

'That was a good story, Sam,' said

Miss Green, rising from her knees and coming over to them.

'It was Scales who told it,' Class 4 corrected her.

'Well, thank you, Scales,' said Miss Green. 'Look what I've found, Class 4, treasure!' She showed them four flat boxes covered with dust. She lifted the lids, and there were board games, all sorts, with dice and counters. 'Tomorrow, if we get our work done, we'll play with them.'

'Promise?' cried Class 4.

'Promise,' said Miss Green.

6 Granny Grubb Grumbles On

'For goodness sake, Ivy Grubb,' said Miss Green sharply, 'put that doll away. Her squeaking is driving me mad. Friday afternoon is toy time, not Tuesday morning.'

'She's not squeaking,' cried Class 4. 'She's saying, "Mama, mama, mama." '

'She shouldn't be talking at all,' said Miss Green, 'when we're all trying to work. She shouldn't be sitting on Ivy's lap. She shouldn't be here.'

'Her name's Sophie,' said Ivy Grubb, tossing her ringlets. 'She's my birthday doll.'

'I know she is your birthday doll,' said Miss Green, 'I know today is your birthday, that is why I very nicely didn't make your Granny take her straight home again this morning, but we are supposed to be working. Put her on top of my cupboard, please.'

So Ivy put Sophie up on the cupboard in a very fussy way, and came back to her seat tossing her hair, fingering her frills and shaking her necklace about. She was a very tossy girl.

When it was playtime Miss Green said, 'Now, Ivy, don't take Sophie out into the playground, because she might get broken.'

'Yes, Miss Green,' said Ivy, but when Miss Green had taken her handbag up to the staffroom, Ivy sneaked back into the classroom and took Sophie out to play.

She walked about the playground carrying Sophie in her arms, surrounded by admiring friends, but when little Tina came up to her and said, 'Please, Ivy, may I hold your beautiful doll?' Ivy said, 'No, you can't. Only my special friends are allowed to hold her' and her special friends closed round her in a tight little ring and shut Tina out. Tina put her finger in her mouth. She had once brought a doll to play with on a Friday afternoon, a rag doll that her mother had

bought at a jumble sale, and Ivy had sneered at it.

'My mother would never let me touch a second-hand toy,' she had said. 'She says you don't know where they've been.'

At dinner-time Miss Green said, 'Now, Ivy, take Sophie home and don't bring her back till Friday. In fact,' went on Miss Green, 'I'd just as soon you didn't bring her back at all, because she's a very expensive doll and if she got . . . Good gracious, Ivy, what's the matter?' For Ivy was letting out shriek after shriek as though someone were emptying ice-cubes down her back.

'Oh,' cried little Tina, bursting into tears, 'oh, she is come to part!'

For there in Ivy's arms was Sophie, without her head.

'Oh, my goodness,' cried poor Miss Green. 'But, Ivy, why are you over by Scales' cave? Wasn't Sophie on top of my cupboard?'

'Please, Miss,' cried Sebastian, jumping up, 'Ivy took Sophie out to play after you'd gone to the staffroom, and when we came in she couldn't put her back on top of the cupboard, because you were already in the classroom, so she pushed her into Scales' cave.'

A sudden horrid thought came to Sam. He went over to Scales' cave and put his hand in. 'Oh, golly,' he groaned, and pulled out Sophie's head. Her blue eyes looked at him in surprise.

'It was my fault,' Sam told Miss Green, talking very quickly to drown Ivy's shrieks and Sebastian's explanations. 'I was tidying Scales' table when I saw Sophie in the cave and tried to pull her out and her head came off and . . .'

'He didn't, he wasn't,' Sebastian shouted, 'Sam never pulled Sophie's head off, Miss Green, it was . . . '

'Be quiet, everybody!' cried Miss Green. 'Ivy, you are *very* naughty. Sebastian, I don't want to hear tales. Sam, you shouldn't have touched

Sophie, she's a very expensive doll. Stop making that noise, Ivy, it won't put Sophie's head on and it's making my head come off. I will write a note to your Granny.'

Ivy went sniffing home to dinner, carrying Sophie, and her head, wrapped in a shawl from the Wendy House, and dropping large tears on Miss Green's note. Miss Green took her handbag up to the staffroom with a very bleak expression, and Sam nipped swiftly over to Scales' cave.

'You shouldn't have done that, Scales,' he whispered. 'You don't know Granny Grubb! She's *grue!*'

'I thought she was meant for me,' said Scales, coming out. 'Honestly, Sam, I thought, oh good, they've brought me a maiden, I'm grown-up at last! But I couldn't swallow her straight down like my dad, her head was too big!'

'You'll have to do something,' said Sam. 'Granny Grubb is terrible!'

Class 4 had hardly settled itself back after dinner when Granny Grubb came marching into the classroom.

'It's very hard on a child if she can't bring a toy to school without it getting broke!' she began.

'That doll should never have been brought to school,' said Miss Green, opening her register.

'You should have kept an eye on it,' said Granny Grubb.

'Ivy was a very disobedient little girl,' said Miss Green. 'Did she tell you what she did?'

'You're the teacher in this class-room, you're responsible,' said Granny

Grubb, who had won many an argument by not listening to the other side. She looked at Tina. 'Our Ivy's too generous, always letting other children play with her nice new toys.'

'Mrs Grubb, I explained what happened in my letter,' said Miss Green. 'We are all very sorry that Sophie is broken, but she should never have been in Scales' cave and you know who put her there.'

'Ha!' snorted Granny Grubb. 'That's not good enough!' And she about-turned and swung briskly off.

Presently, Miss Barley opened the door and Class 4 saw Granny Grubb behind her in the corridor.

'Could you come out for a minute, please, Miss Green?' said Miss Barley in her quiet voice.

So Miss Green went out and Class 4 could hear Granny Grubb grumbling on. Then the door opened again and Miss Barley said, 'Ivy dear, will you come out for a moment, please?' And Ivy went out and Class 4 heard

Granny Grubb's voice grumbling on. Miss Green opened the door next and looked across at Sam.

'Sam, just come out for a minute, please.'

So Sam went out, and the door closed, and Class 4 heard Miss Barley's quiet voice, and Miss Green's firm one, and Sam and Ivy both talking together, but through them all, they heard Granny Grubb's voice grumbling on.

'What a silly carry-on,' said Scales at the end of the day. 'It won't put her head back on. I'm jolly glad I bit it off. I only wish I'd been able to swallow it.'

The next day was glum. Granny Grubb rumbled round the corridors like a storm looking for somewhere to burst. Miss Green looked as though she were getting one of her headaches. Ivy was more tossy than ever, and little Tina seemed shrunken with sadness.

At playtime Sam went over to the

dustbins. They seemed comfortingly solid after all the squalls in the class-room.

'Psst!' hissed Scales, appearing round them. 'Go and get Tina and Ivy.'

'Together?' asked Sam. 'Ivy won't come with Tina.'

'Tell her I love her,' said Scales, 'because she's bossy and frilly like a dragon.'

Sam found Tina comforting one of the baby class who had fallen over. 'Scales wants you,' he said. Then he pulled Ivy out of her circle of special friends. 'Scales wants to see you,' he told her. 'He likes your frills.' He led them over to the dustbins.

'Crouch down,' hissed Scales. 'I don't want anyone else to see. Aunt Spiny's sent these for you.'

He lifted his wings and two little dragons fell down. The girls gasped and backed away. The little dragons lay there, unmoving, unblinking. 'They're dolls,' breathed Ivy, 'beautiful,

beautiful dragon dolls.' Tina said nothing, but her little face shone like a star.

Scales gave the bigger to Ivy. 'It's a bit worn,' he said. 'It belonged to my eldest cousin, but she doesn't play with it any more. The little one is for you,' he said, turning to Tina. 'It's brand new. My mum made it for my youngest cousin, but Aunt Spiny says she's got enough toys.'

'But what shall we tell our mums?' asked Ivy.

'Say my mum made them,' said Sam. 'She does do sewing, sometimes.'

'That's clever,' said Ivy, tossing her ringlets, 'because my nan knows that your mum's clever. Come on, Tina, let's go and play with them. Mine shall be the mother, and yours can be the baby.' They ran off, and Sam heard them bending the dragon dolls forwards and back to make them hiss. He would have liked a present himself, though he didn't want a doll. Scales put something hard, cold and spiky into his hand.

'You remember the man who came up our mountain? He was so grateful to Aunt Spiny for sparing his life that when he got home he took his sword-hilt to a bronze-smith and had it melted down and made into that little dragon, and sent it up the mountain to our cave as a peace-offering.'

'It's scary,' said Sam, looking down at the open jaws. 'It's so real it looks as if it would bite. Is it your dad?'

'My dad, no!' said Scales. 'My dad never looks like that. That's my Aunt Spiny to the life. She's very fond of it, but she's sent it for Granny Grubb as a peace-offering because I spoilt Sophie.'

'For Granny Grubb!' echoed Sam.

'Yes,' said Scales. 'My Aunt Spiny thinks well of Granny Grubb. A female's first duty is to defend her young! And she *liked* the way Granny Grubb went straight up to Miss Green and bit her head off.'

7 Brave Boys and Daring Damsels

' "Tobay is Monbay"?' read out Miss Green. ' "I went for a walk with my bad and we took our bog"? Oh, Sam, what am I going to do with you?'

'Rotten old *b* and *d*,' said Sam, 'I always muddle them.'

'Ah well, you're not the only one,' said Miss Green. She stood up. 'Television time? Plug the television in, please, Christopher. Now, Class 4,

I'm going into the bay to finish marking your newsbooks, so sit quietly and watch!' She moved away and Class 4 settled down on the magic mat. Scales came out of his cave. He loved television.

Sam went over to him. 'I never remember which way round a *b* goes,' he moaned. 'I always get it wrong.'

'Ssh!' said Scales, staring at the television. Sam frowned at the picture.

'Today we're going to make a woodpecker,' said the smiling young lady, and dissolved into dots! 'Please, Miss, the telly's br . . . ' began Sebastian.

'Ssh,' said Scales, staring harder than ever at the set. The dots were different colours, blue, purple, brown, grey. The different colours began to run about and find each other.

'Oh, it's . . . ' began Class 4.

'Ssh,' said Scales, staring. A new picture began to show as the different-coloured dots joined together, a path going up a mountainside. The brown dots that made up the path went on busily joining together, even after the heather and rocks and boulders and grass were finished.

'Oh, it's coming,' began Sam.

'Ssh,' said Scales, staring at the path. The end nearest to him went on growing. A smell of cold air came out of the television, purple heather pricked Sam's legs, the path touched the magic mat. Scales hopped on to it. 'Follow me,' he said quietly. Bubbling with excitement, but quiet as mice, Class 4 followed.

My, it was cold! Yet in a few moments they were warm as toast. Class 4 had never seen a hill, let alone climbed a mountain, before. The flat fen country lay like a mat for miles around the school. But now they were dancing up the path, jumping over rocks and boulders as though they had springs in their legs.

'Better than making woodpeckers,' chuckled Billy Bottom. 'Cor, look at that!' And he pointed to a tall rock, with a round boulder with a hole in it pressed against its right-hand side. It blocked the path. 'It's got writing on it,' cried Billy. 'Come on up, Chris, and read it.'

' "B-b-boys b-b-beware!" ' read Christopher, panting. ' "Beware" means "look out"!'

'Oo-er!' said Class 4, biting its nails.

'I'm not scared,' said Billy boastfully, and he bent his bullet head and bulldozed through the hole. 'Ow, I've bumped my head. The roof bulges.'

So Class 4 bent its head and crawled through carefully and saw Scales bounding ahead. The path got steeper. Billy began to blow like a grampus, and dainty Dinny Delmont took the lead, her red pigtails dancing on her shoulders.

'Here's another of 'em!' she screeched. 'Only the round bit's on the other side!'

A mountain stream cut across the path with a racing hurry and clatter and in the middle of it stood another tall rock with a boulder leaning against it, but this time on the left-hand side.

'It's got a hole in it, too, and writing!' screeched Dinny. And she leant forward and read, ' "Damsels desist!" Damsels desist? What's that mean?'

'Damsels are girls,' Sam said.

'Desist means stop,' said clever Christopher.

'Oo-er!' said Class 4 doubtfully.

'Doesn't mean me!' said Dinny defiantly, and jumped. Her dungarees disappeared into the dark hole. They heard her shout 'Done it!' And saw her standing on the opposite bank. 'Come on, you lot, you can do it!'

So Class 4 did it, and saw Scales darting ahead of them. The path rushed on to the top and Class 4 rushed up it, Billy and Dinny racing for the lead. Over the top and – Billy and Dinny both stopped dead.

'Oo-er!' said Class 4.

Facing them was a cave with two rock-and-boulder shapes, one on either side, with the letter b carved on one and the letter d carved on the other, and looking at them with a smile that

seemed to go on for ever, it had so many teeth in it, was – a dragon.

'Damsels through *d*, boys through *b*,' hissed the dragon. 'Damsels I dip in dripping, boys I baste with butter. Damsels,' it went on dreamily, 'are delicious for dinner. Boys are best for breakfast.'

'What does "baste" mean?' asked Christopher, who had to know, although his knees were knocking together.

'Spooning the fat over the meat to stop it from drying out,' said the dragon.

'Don't be silly, Aunt Spiny,' cried Scales, coming out of the cave. 'This is Class 4 that I've told you about. You know them!'

'Bless my spines, nephew, but I mistook them for real children.'

'They are real children and you don't eat children anyway. You know you don't.'

'Not these children anyroad,' agreed the old dragon, touching her cold nose to Weefy Buffalo's sparrow legs.

Weefy's mouth fell open. 'Shut it up, youngling, fresh air won't fatten you. You've ten years growing to do, before you make a meal. There, that's just my joke. I like a joke with a bite to it.'

'Come and meet my mum,' called Scales. 'She's making rock cakes.' But Class 4 hung back.

'Come on,' cried Billy and Dinny. 'Aunt Spiny won't eat us!' And they smiled at the old dragon as they moved forward.

But once inside the cave no-one could feel frightened, there was so much warmth and glow. A big dragon was baking cakes at the fire with her back to them. 'Mum,' cried Scales, 'here's Class 4 and Sam, that I keep telling you about.'

'What a nice Class 4, what a lovely Sam,' murmured the big dragon without turning round.

'You're not looking,' complained Scales, 'turn round, Mum.'

'Not now, dear, I'm busy,' said the big dragon. 'Take these rock cakes and call your cousins.'

'Can Class 4 have some?'

'When your cousins have had theirs.'

Then Class 4 saw, peeping from every crack, cranny and crevice in the cave, little dragons watching them with amazed black eyes in which the firelight winked. Scales put the rock cakes on the table, whispering, 'Take yours first' to Class 4, and called, 'Rock cakes ready! Meet my silly cousins.' All the little dragons rushed for the table and sat round it, staring at Class 4 as though they were seeing marvels.

The rock cakes were hot, curranty and spicy. Aunt Spiny came into the cave to help. 'Aunt Spiny,' said Scales, 'can you make Sam remember which way a b goes?'

'Pat your belly,' snapped Aunt Spiny. Sam patted his tummy and giggled. 'Where's your belly? At the back or at the front?'

'At the front,' giggled Sam.

'That's where the belly is in b,' growled Aunt Spiny. She picked a charred stick out of the fire and drew a big, black b on the wall. 'Belly in front. Remember it!' How lovely to live in a cave and draw on the walls, thought Sam. 'More spice,' muttered Aunt Spiny, and went waddling off down the cave.

'What about *d*?' called Dinny. She's daring, thought Sam.

Aunt Spiny's voice came from the darkness, 'I'll show you a *d*,' she rasped.

Dinny jumped up and darted after her, but the further she went, the slower her footsteps got. It was dim and shadowy beyond the circle of firelight, colder too. There were darkways and doorways that she did not quite like, humps and bumps that might be one thing or might be another. Her eyes made out a straight black line standing up ahead of her and halfway down it on the left-hand side a hunched black shape. A warning rang in her brain. 'Danger! Don't go!' She hesitated. She was a long way from the fire and Scales and safety. A claw scraped. There was a dry hiss. Dinny turned and fled.

Aunt Spiny straightened up, shut the cupboard door and came waddling back with a jar of spice in her claw. 'Very wise of you,' she said dryly to Dinny as she passed. She picked up the stick and wrote d on the wall and turned it into a little picture. 'Dragon behind the door! Danger! Don't forget it!'

A rumbling began, a shaking, all the little dragons scurried to their hiding places. 'There's your father coming, Scales,' said his mother. 'Tidy up now, put away your drawing.'

Aunt Spiny seized a broom and began sweeping up, muttering, 'Better be off, don't delay, better be safe, on your way.' The broom came nearer and nearer. Class 4 felt itself whisked out of the cave, down the mountainside and into the classroom, just as the bell rang for playtime.

'I say,' giggled Billy Bottom, 'Miss is never going to believe our stories when we write them!'

But, strange to say, Miss did! 'Every word, Billy! You make it sound so real. But what I can't believe is that all of you, even Sam, have got every *b* and *d* the right way round!'

'Goob!' said Sam.

8 Scales and the Snowmen

Harvest Festival had been and gone. The tins from Tesco and the vegetable marrows had been given to the Old People's Home and term was rushing towards Christmas like a snowball to a face.

'Scales will love Christmas,' said Sam. 'It's so bright and sparkly, just like Scales himself!'

'Scales can't be in Christmas!' said Miss Green. 'There are no dragons in

Christmas and, besides, we need his table for the crib. Scales will have to go into the bay. He can go by the radiator and hibernate till Spring.' And she told Sam and Christopher to carry Scales' cave into the bay. The bay was stuffed with things that had been banished to make way for Christmas.

'He won't like it here,' said Sam. 'He won't see anybody.'

'I don't like it,' said Christopher. 'It doesn't seem fair.'

'We'll come and see you,' they said to Scales.

'You'd better,' said Scales. 'I shall shrivel up if I don't get P and G.'

'What's P and G?'

'Praise and Glory,' said Scales. 'Attention. Everyone saying you're great! All dragons must have it, me more than most.'

They went back to the classroom, where Miss Barley was handing a box to Miss Green.

'Coloured foil, glitter, tissue paper circles, cottonwool, card and calendar tags. Thank you, Miss Green!' She smiled at them and went out. Christmas had begun.

'We'll do some cottonwool snowmen on our cards,' said Miss Green, 'with snowflakes behind them.'

'If we can't get Scales into Christmas,' Sam told Billy, 'he'll shrivel up.'

'Like a bit of old bootleather,' said Billy. 'Let's moan at Miss till she lets him in. I moan at our Mum and she gives in.'

So they did, but Miss Green did not give in. 'But if you moan at me any more you *will* have a dragon in Christmas. Me!' And she pulled a fearsome face.

As the busy days went by Class 4 forgot about Scales. Sam remembered him sometimes. Then, even Sam forgot.

One afternoon the sky turned yellow. 'Br-r-r!' shivered Miss Green. 'It's cold. Look at that sky!'

Class 4 looked and went instantly mad. 'Snow!' they shrieked, rushing

to the window. Snow it was. Magical
beautiful snow. By playtime the yard
was white with it, by hometime the
flakes were falling so thickly the
mums came with extra wraps for the
little ones and cars had their head-
lights on. By next morning it was so
deep that Class 4 came in wellies
which left blue holes in the snow.

I lik snow cos you put pople's fas in it,

wrote Billy Bottom in his newsbook.

I hat snow because it maks mi feet wet and peple put my fas in it,

wrote Weefy Buffalo.

Miss Barley announced a snowman competition. Each class was to have its own patch. Class 4's was under the bay.

Miss Green put plastic bags over Class 4's gloved and mittened hands to keep them dry and secured them with elastic bands. 'But no-one is to put anyone's face in the snow, or I shall put their face back in the class-room!' Sam went to Class 5 to borrow the spades from their sandtray, and out they marched, but when they came round to the bay—no snow!

'Where's it gone?' cried Class 4

staring. It was everywhere else, but not by their bay. 'That's strange,' said Miss Green. 'Why has it melted here and nowhere else? Is it warmer by our bay? Never mind! By the colour of that sky there's more snow to come.'

She was right. Next morning the yard looked like the top of a Christmas cake before the decorations go on. Class 4 got into its clobber again, Miss Green elastic-banded the plastic bags again, and Sam asked Class 5 for their spades again. 'Good luck,' said Class 5, 'but you won't beat our snowman! He's huge!'

'Course we'll beat him,' said Billy Bottom. 'We'll build a snowman big as Miss!'

And off they marched. Along the corridor, down the steps, round the corner, and up to the bay. No snow! Snow everywhere else, but by the bay slush and steaming puddles. Sam stared at the puddles. He took off his plastic bag and glove and dipped his finger in one of them. The puddle was warm.

'Someone's stealing our snow,' said Class 4.

'Well, we musn't steal anyone else's,' said Miss Green. 'It's got to be our snowman on our patch, or not at all.'

'Bad luck,' said Class 5, 'but did you see our snowman? He's the best.'

Sam went thoughtfully back to the classroom. It was full of cross children taking things off and getting in each other's way and a bright red Miss Green pulling off plastic bags and elastic bands. Sam slipped through them into the bay. He had to wriggle on his tummy to get to Scales' cave.

'Is it you, Scales? Are you cross, because we forgot you? Are you laying wasting our snow?'

He could hardly hear Scales' reply.

'Must have P and G, Sam. Must. Nearly gone, Sam.'

'Oh, Scales, don't go! Don't go! Hang on!'

'Miss Green,' cried Sam, 'we *must* have Scales in Christmas, or he'll disappear!'

'Oh, Sam, I've told you,' said Miss Green, handing out tissue paper circles for puffballs, 'dragons don't belong in Christmas and there isn't room.'

'We have mistletoe and holly and yule logs in Christmas,' said clever Christopher. 'My father says they're from pagan times long before Jesus was born. Why don't we make Scales a winter sunfeast in the bay?'

'Yes,' cried Class 4, 'let's make Scales a winter sunfeast in the bay!'

'We could clear a space and put his cave on a table by the window,' said Christopher.

'Our holly tree's got berries on it,' said Sebastian. 'I'll bring him a branch.'

'I've got a giant fircone at home,' said Weefy Buffalo, 'I'll glitter it for him.'

'The first puffball I make,' said Ivy Grubb, 'I'll hang over his cave.'

'I will make him a special card,' said tiny Tina.

'My mum's bought a packet of

icicles, I'll put them over Scales' cave,' said Billy Bottom.

'We'll write Happy Sunfeast, Scales, in cottonwool across his window,' said Miss Green, 'and we'll do it now!' And she went into the bay with Sam and Christopher, big strong Billy and deft Dinny Delmont, and shifted and shunted till they had made a space for Scales. Then they heaved his cave up into the sunlight and blew the dust off it.

'Turn it to face the sun,' said Christopher.

'This is a good idea of yours, Christopher,' said Miss Green. 'We all love Scales ('and he loves us,' said Dinny) and we shouldn't cast out love from Christmas, because love is what it's all about.'

That night more snow fell and next morning all the snowmen had new white coats on.

'Can we have another try at our snowman?' asked Sam.

'Sam, there isn't time. Miss Barley is judging the snowmen at playtime,' said Miss Green, who was standing on a chair putting up puffballs.

'Even the baby class has made a snowman,' said Billy.

'Not all that dressing up *again*,' groaned Weefy.

'P-l-e-a-s-e,' pleaded Sam and Billy and Dinny.

'I must be mad,' said Miss Green, getting down. 'One last try! Tog up, everybody! Sam, nip up to Class 5 for their spades.'

'What, again?' laughed Class 5. 'Why don't you give up? We're going to win.'

Class 4 humped itself into its coats, Miss Green got out the plastic bags and elastic bands and they lumbered out like a badtempered crocodile complaining in all its joints. 'There won't be any snow,' said Ivy Grubb, tossing her head. 'It'll all be melted like it was yesterday and the day before, you silly Sam Luckett.' Down the steps they stumped, round the corner they trudged and
                    'SNOW!'

they yelled, for there under the bay was a shining sheet of untouched snow.

Who won the prize? Class 5 did. Their snowman was the best. But Class 4 got a special mention from Miss Barley. 'I don't think a class has ever built a snow*dragon* before. It's most original. I shall telephone the newspapers to come and photograph it.'

All that afternoon people kept coming to admire the snowdragon. Dinner ladies, cleaners, big brothers and sisters from the Juniors, even the

Headmaster himself. 'I can believe in that dragon,' said one photographer. 'He's great!'

Sam and Christopher turned at the gate for a last look. The low winter sun was slanting across the playground, turning the bay window and the dragon that sat there to gold. Scales was looking down at his snow statue.

'I can see his grin from here,' said Christopher. 'He won't go away! He's puffed up with P and G. You were clever, Sam, to work out what was happening.'

'You were jolly clever, Chris, to get Miss Green to let him into Christmas.'

'We were clever to build that snow-dragon!'

And they went home, puffed up with P and G.

9 Sebastian's Mum Puts Her Foot In It

So Scales was allowed into Christmas, but he didn't look happy. 'I thought you'd be pleased,' said Sam. 'You don't look pleased.'

'I'm deaf,' said Scales. 'My cousins keep going on at me.'

'What are they going on about?'

'They want to come to the Christmas Party. Ever since you came to our cave, they've been wild to visit Class 4.'

'How many cousins have you?' asked Sam.

'Twenty!' said Scales gloomily. 'Aunt Spiny counts them every night.'

They were sitting in the bay decorating hoops for the hall. Sam watched as Scales tied holly branches to the rim of a red hoop and hung gold bells made from milk bottle tops from the leaves. 'That's brilliant, Scales,' he said. An idea struck him. He leant forward and whispered in Scales' ear.

'Course they'd have to be dead still and quiet. Do you think they could?'

'They'd be dead if they were,' grunted Scales, but he looked pleased.

Jennie the Helper came in for more hoops. 'That's a pretty one,' she said. 'Who made it?'

'Scales,' said Sam. 'He's clever with his claws.'

'Shall we do it then?' Sam asked. Scales nodded. 'I'll tell the others, then,' said Sam. He whispered into Billy's ear. 'Pass it on!'

Jennie came back for more hoops. 'These are a bit skimpy! Can't you put more in the middle?'

'We haven't got much stuff,' said Sam. 'They'll look all right when they're hung up.'

Party morning came. Class 4 brought tins of fruit and homemade cakes, chocolate biscuits and packets of jelly. Miss Green disappeared into the staffroom to make jellies. Sebastian, who was delivering Christmas cards, kept popping back to report: 'Jennie's in the stockroom wrapping up things! Miss Barley's putting a white sheet over the coffee trolley. She's sprinkling glitter on it!'

Afternoon play was double length, because Miss Barley, Miss Green and Jennie were flying around the hall setting out the tea, putting a coloured candle in the middle of every table. Across the corridor, Scales watched them with his eye glued to a crack in the classroom door. 'Now,' said Miss Barley, 'that's fair shares for all. Let's have a cup of tea before the children come in. Come along, Miss Green, lock the doors, Jennie.' Jennie locked the folding doors and followed them. But what are locked doors to a dragon who is clever with his claws?

The bell went. Class 4 streamed in, buzzing with excitement. The girls got into party dresses, the boys (some of them) into clean shirts, and all trooped to the Music Room, where Miss Barley, who knew more games than anyone and had an eagle eye for cheats, was waiting.

When they were gasping, with not

a breath left, she held up her hand and said, 'Tea!' and led them, giggling and jiggling, into the hall, where kind mums were waiting to help.

'Aren't the hoops lovely, Miss Barley!' cried the mums. 'However did the children fill them so full?' For the hoops were filled to the rim with brilliant bright and prickly things.

'Too heavy!' murmured Sebastian's mother, a tiresome woman. 'They could come down!'

'Mrs Brown, perhaps you could start taking the sandwiches round?' said Miss Barley.

'Look at that dragon on the wallbars behind Sam Luckett's head! He's eating a cake!' gasped Sebastian's mother, dropping the sandwiches.

'Now, Mrs Brown,' said Mrs Barley, 'don't get excited or you'll set the children off. It's just the light playing on its scales that makes it look alive.'

Sam grinned and passed another cake to Scales.

Gradually the eating got slower, the mums ceased to swoop from table to table with their cries of 'Any more jelly?' Miss Green stopped pouring orange, and the children saw that Miss Barley was standing by the door with her hand to her ear.

'Listen!' she said. Faint and silvery came the sound of sleigh bells. A whisper ran round the hall. 'Father Christmas is coming!' 'Don't stir,' said Miss Barley. 'Don't even breathe! Miss Green and I will go and see if it's true.' She stole out. Miss Green followed. The lights went out. Jennie scurried round lighting the candles. Music began. The sleighbells rang nearer. All eyes stared at the door. Class 4 raised its hand and twenty little dragons glided down from the hoops and settled on the Class 4 tables. The music swelled, the sleigh bells rang loud and clear, the children shouted. Beneath the noise twenty little dragons gobbled up the cakes on the Class 4 tables, while the candle flames bent this way and that.

'There's a dragon on your plate!' shrieked Sebastian's Mum. 'Sebastian, there's a dra—'

'Hush now, you and your dragons!' said the mum beside her. 'Father Christmas is coming.'

Jennie clashed the cymbals. Class 4 waved their party hats in the air, and twenty little dragons soared up-wards as Father Christmas came through the door on a snow-covered sleigh pulled by laughing Miss Barley, pushed by panting Miss Green, and nobody noticed the hoops swaying wildly above or the crumbs floating down.

Then Class 4 were going up to receive a pink or blue wrapped present, the mums were watching with pride and love, and no-one was listening to Mrs Brown saying, '*Little dragons . . .*'

Then it was over, and Miss Barley was saying, 'Children with mothers here can go straight home. Jennie will open the side door at the top of the hall. The rest get your coats and come to the Music Room.'

Children with mums filed out by the side door, children without mums went off to sing carols, Jennie put out the candles and went away. The hall was silent and dark.

For a bit.

Then eyes began to glow in the hoops above, rustling and whirrings sounded, while over by the wallbars something slipped to the floor and said: 'Now then, sillies, the party's over. Flit off home before Aunt Spiny starts counting!'

But the little dragons squeaked, 'We want our take-home cake! Class 4 had take-home cake. We saw them.' And they scuttered about the hall, snatching at pink and blue paper, and fluttered over the tables looking for leftover cakes. They pulled bits of tinsel off the wallbars to tie up the cakes and hung them round each other's necks. Some of the parcels came undone and they had to start again. Scales went frantic. 'Get on, get on!' he hissed, flinging some out of the side door like so many fireworks.

Far away a voice was counting. 'One, Two, Three. Four? Four, Five . . .'

Scales scooted back for more cousins. 'Come on, leave that!' He flung another bunch out. The voice had a rasp to it. 'Six, Seven, Eight? Oh, Eight! Nine, Ten . . .'

Scales was spanking his little cousins off the tables, picking up dropped cakes, tying on bundles for all he was worth.

'I should never have let you into

Christmas. I knew you'd be too silly. If you've dropped it, you've dropped it. Oh, all right, here you are, now *go!*'

Such a trail of bright sparks leaving the open side door!

'Eleven, Twelve. Come along, Thirteen, Fourteen . . . '

In bunches and singly the little dragons whizzed into the night. Some of them stopped to kiss Scales. 'Thank you for our lovely party!'

'Get on, get *on*,' moaned Scales. 'Don't start kissing, for goodness sake.'

'Fifteen, Sixteen, Seventeen . . . '

Two more little dragons flew past him.

'Eighteen, Nineteen . . . '

One more. Scales looked round. The littlest dragon was sitting on the floor trying desperately to tie up a butterfly cake in a piece of pink paper very much torn.

'Scoot!' cried Scales. 'Aunt Spiny's up to Nineteen!'

'I'm wrapping up my take-home cake,' squeaked the littlest dragon.

Scales started forward to help. The lights went on. Scales flattened himself against the wallbars. Sebastian's Mum came into the hall. 'Where did I put my handbag . . . oh!' The littlest dragon gave a roar of grief.

'You've treaded on my take-home cake! Now I'll be late and my Mum will hit me and . . . '

'Oh, never you roar like that, my duck,' cried Sebastian's Mum. 'Here's some more paper. Here's a fresh cake. Here's a chocolate biscuit. Now, you give the biscuit to your Mam and she won't hit you! She's not a dragon.' And with fingers that had fixed many a bow tie round Sebastian's neck, Mrs Brown made a neat little parcel and hung it round the littlest dragon's neck. Then her eye fell on her handbag and she picked it up. The littlest dragon flew off, slowly, rather wobbly, but *going*!

Sebastian's Mum wiped the mess off her shoe and stared about her. Scales was leaning lopsidedly against the wallbars. 'I'll not say anything,' she murmured. 'They'd only laugh.'

Jennie came back to clear the tables.

'Would you believe it? Not a crumb left! Usually there's enough for us to have another feast tomorrow!'

'Ah, but you had extra mouths this year!'

'Extra mouths?' asked Jennie, 'Whatever do you mean?'

She began to walk up the hall to the side door. The faraway voice sounded angry. 'Twenty? Twenty? You *naughty* little . . . Oh! For me, dear?

Thank you.' Jennie shut the door with a snap and drew the curtains.

'How many extra mouths, Mrs Brown?'

'Twenty,' said Sebastian's Mum. She looked at Scales. 'No! Twenty-one.'

10 *The Last Thing Dragons Do*

The day that would *never* come, came!
The last day of term! Class 4 brought
their favourite toys to play with while
Miss Green finished tidying. Sam
brought his treasures in the yellow
Singapore Airport plastic bag with
the Chinese writing on it, and he and
Weefy went into the bay to look at
them. There was a flint arrowhead
from Cockley Cley, a huge, empty,
polished snailshell, striped brown

and white like a humbug, in which a French snail had once lived, a man made out of horseshoe nails, a carrot that looked like two men wrestling, and a fierce dark dragon made out of melted-down swordhilts. They played until Miss Green called 'Dustbins!' when they leaped up and ran to join the glorious end-of-term procession to the dustbins.

Out went wall pictures faded and torn, out went models broken and battered, out went charts filled up and finished with, until the classroom was as bare as a winter tree. Then Miss Green lifted the Class 4 Christmas Tree on to her desk and got out her big scissors. Snap went the scissors. 'Catch,' called Miss Green and a parcel flew through the air. Snap, snap, snap! Faster and faster flew the parcels until the tree was bare. Inside were funny rubbers, funny pencils, funny sharpeners, funny balloons, but no sweets. 'Because of your teeth,' said Miss Green.

In came the Christmas Postman

with an invitation for Tina to Ivy Grubb's Christmas Party. In came Jennie the helper with the Christmas cake which Class 4 had mixed. In came Class 1 with mince pies they'd baked themselves. 'I don't eat mince pies,' said Weefy Buffalo. 'I don't like Christmas cake!'

Then it was Assembly. 'Take care on the roads,' said Miss Barley. 'I want you all back next term with all your arms and legs on and your brain safe inside your heads and not left on a road somewhere.'

Then it was over and Sam was struggling up the lane with his PE kit and his picture that won a gold star and his model of a lightship and his grapefruit tree in a yoghurt pot, and a bag with the Christmas Card and Calendar for his mother.

Dusk was deepening into dark, birds were rustling in the brown hedgerows, the baby swings hung empty in the muddy rec. It was drab cold winter, but excitement tingled in the air, for behind the grey chill the red fires of Christmas were drawing near.

It wasn't until Sam was shedding his burdens on the kitchen table that he made the awful discovery.

'What is it?' cried his mother.

'My treasures!' wailed Sam. 'I've left them at school!' He turned and ran out of the door and had reached the gate when his mother caught him. She had thrown her coat on over her apron and was on her bike.

'Go back in the warm, I've poured your tea. I'll get them. Tell me where you were playing.'

'In the bay. They were in my Singapore bag.'

'I'll get them,' said his mother.

But when she came back she hadn't got them.

'I've searched everywhere, but I couldn't see your Singapore bag.'

'I'll go down and look,' cried Sam. 'I should have gone down to look, not you.'

'Now don't *worry*,' said his mum. 'Mr Duffy says you can go down tomorrow and search the dustbins.'

She opened the cake tin, pinned up his picture, watered the grapefruit tree, but nothing could take the chill from Sam's heart. Supposing Mr Duffy took the carrot home for supper? Supposing one of the cleaning ladies stepped on the snailshell, not knowing that a French snail had lived there?

As soon as he'd swallowed his cereal he was racing down to school next morning. Mr Duffy let him in. 'Seeing as it's you, Sam Luckett. I know you're worried. Your poor Ma was here last night. Have a look in the dustbins, but mind you put everything back. Then take a gander round the classroom.'

'A gander?' said Sam.

'A look,' said Mr Duffy.

Sam searched the dustbins. Chalk dust and dried paint settled on his clothes, bits of old Sellotape stuck to his hands. He found some interesting throwouts, but he couldn't find his Singapore bag. Mr Duffy whistled when he saw him. 'You'd better have a wash before you go home,' he said. 'Go and look in the bay now, but be quick.'

Sam went into the bay and stared. Everything had been folded up, taken down and covered over. He didn't know where to start looking, let alone how to be quick. The awful certainty that he would never see his treasures again hit him like a hammer blow. His throat swelled with misery. He sat down on a box and began to cry. Scales came out from somewhere and looked at him.

'What's up Sam?'

'I've lost my treasures,' gulped Sam.

Scales looked smug. 'What's the third thing dragons do, Sam?'

Sam sniffed. 'They devour maidens, they lay waste, they— they— I've forgotten what the third thing is.'

'Dragons don't forget,' said Scales. 'Hop on my back.'

'Mr Duffy'll see,' sniffed Sam.

'Mr Duffy's having his coffee,' said Scales. 'Come to the top of the steps where I can get a good take-off.'

Sam followed him down the corridor to the back steps, wedged himself between two spines, and whoosh! the school ran away below them and they were hurtling through the air. Sam closed his eyes against the rush and glitter. Then his stomach came up into his mouth and scrunch! they were down. He opened his eyes, got off and found his legs trembling.

The dragons' cave looked empty. 'Good,' said Scales. 'They're out. Come in.' The fire was white soft ash, the baking rock was empty, but the b and d that Aunt Spiny had drawn with the charcoal stick were still on the wall.

'Over here,' said Scales, crossing the cave. 'Up here,' he called, running up a wall. 'Through here,' he puffed. Sam climbed up the wall. It wasn't so easy for him, he didn't have four sets of claws! When he came to the place where Scales had disappeared, he found a narrow crack that he could *just* squeeze through. 'Down here,' came Scales' voice. 'Let yourself go, it's all right,' It didn't feel all right, it was pitch black, but Sam let himself go and landed with a soft bump. A red glow sprang up and Class 4 crowded round him.

'Golly,' he cried, staring at Class 4. Scales lifted the lamp he had just lit. 'Good, aren't they?' he said. 'I painted them myself. Here's Weefy with his mouth open, Sebastian with his bow tie, Dinny with her pigtails, *beautiful* frilly Ivy Grubb; Christopher looking clever, big Billy, tiny Tina . . . '

'Where am I?' asked Sam.

122

Scales turned round. 'Over here. You were the one I drew first,' he said. 'I drew you on the Samrock to guard my most secret place.' Then Sam saw himself, drawn very brave and tall on a piece of rock quite separate from the others. 'Hold this,' said Scales, giving him the lamp, and began scrabbling with his claws round the edge of the picture. The

lamp jumped in Sam's hand as the Samrock swung slowly outwards and revealed a shining yellow heap behind it.

'It's my hoard,' panted Scales. 'I haven't got much yet, but it'll grow.' He pulled some things out.

'That's the third thing dragons do!' cried Sam, as he bent down and pulled out his yellow Singapore Airport plastic bag with the Chinese writing. 'They guard treasure!'

'It's *the* thing dragons do,' said Scales. 'It's what dragons are *for*.'

There came a heavy tramping. Scales pushed the Samrock shut. 'Quick, Sam, blow out the lamp and follow me.' Sam blew out the lamp. He heard Scales scuttle off and splash into water. He followed and found himself walking in a shallow stream that presently squeezed itself out on to the mountainside.

Scales was shaking the drops off his wings in the bright sunlight.

'Quick,' he said. 'Get on.'

Sam held on tight with both knees

and one hand. The wind iced his cheeks, the sun made rainbows on his eyelashes. Then his stomach was rushing up into his mouth, but not out of it, and he was tumbling off Scales' back into the bay. Scales had disappeared. Mr Duffy was turning off the taps at the sink and looking down at him over his mop and pail.

'Marvellous, isn't it? Leave a boy alone five minutes and he'll make a mess! Wet shoes, splashed trousers! I don't know. Well, I see you found it. Where was it?'

'In Scales' cave!' cried Sam, waving the Singapore bag at him. 'He was guarding it for me!'

'Was he now?' said Mr Duffy. 'Well, I'm glad you found it. Now your poor Ma can enjoy Christmas. Off you go then. I'll put the things back.'

Sam went off beaming. Outside in the yard below the bay he stopped to check his treasures. Out of the empty snailshell fell a gold cloak pin with two dragons shaped like a double S climbing up it. Double SS for Sam and Scales! Scales was looking down at him through the window, yawning sleepily. Sam held the pin up.

'For me?'

Scales nodded.

'Oh, *thanks*!' said Sam, sticking it in his coat. 'What a morning!' Scales sank down into a dragon sleep and shut his eyes tight. Sam swung the Singapore bag up to his shoulder and waved his hand.

'See you, Scales!'

'See you, Sam!'

THE END

A DRAGON IN SPRING-TERM

by June Counsel

'Here we are,' cried Scales cheerfully. 'Spring on Magic Mountain!'

Sam and his friends in Class 4 have a very special friend – a young dragon called Scales. They are all looking forward to seeing him again when they go back to school for the Spring term. But Miss Green, their teacher, has put his cage away in the stockroom and firmly tells the class that this term they will be doing new things starting with a computer . . .

However, all dragons wake up in the Spring, and soon Scales is back with Sam and his friends, leading them all up to Magic Mountain for a series of wonderful adventures!

0 440 862094

YEARLING BOOKS

A DRAGON IN SUMMER

by June Counsel

'Summer term, Sam,' Scales beamed, *'and I'm in it!'*

Sam bounces back to school for the Summer term, looking forward to seeing his special friend Scales again. But will Scales, a young dragon, *want* to be in the term when he hears that Sam's class are going to act out a pageant of St George and the Dragon – and the dragon gets killed?

Luckily Scales knows the story of St George too, although *his* story has a very different ending, and he is determined to share in the fun. Soon Scales is right in the middle of all the excitement, bringing his silly little cousins along to watch the pageant, and whisking Sam and his friends off to Wish Wood and an enchanted island for a series of super adventures!

'A delight of lords and ladies, dragons and castles, witches and magic . . . highly recommended' *Recent Children's Fiction*

0 440 862949

YEARLING BOOKS